This Ladybird book

belongs to

_____

Published by Ladybird Books Ltd
27 Wrights Lane London W8 5TZ
A Penguin Company
2 4 6 8 10 9 7 5 3
© LADYBIRD BOOKS LTD MM
LADYBIRD and the device of a Ladybird are trademarks of Ladybird Books Ltd

Printed in Italy

Little Chick

by Mandy Ross
illustrated by Sarah Gibb

Ladybird

"Snuggle up, little one," said Feathery Hen to Little Chick. And there in the henhouse, cosy and snug, she tucked him under her wing, in a warm feathery hug.

"Feathery wings are so snuggly," cheeped Little Chick. "How do other animals manage without them?"

So (after the snuggle) he went to find out.

First he met Chestnut Foal galloping round the paddock.

"Has your mum got feathery wings for snuggling?" asked Little Chick.

"No, she hasn't!" said Chestnut Foal...

"But when we curl up in the stable, cosy and snug, she blows down my nose in a warm horsey hug."

Next Little Chick met Velvety
Calf munching in the meadow.

"Has your mum got feathery
wings for snuggling?" asked
Little Chick.

"No, she hasn't!"
said Velvety Calf...

*"But when we curl up in the cowshed,
cosy and snug,
she nuzzles my neck in a
warm jersey hug."*

Next Little Chick met
Tabby Kitten chasing around in
the garden.

"Has your mum got feathery
wings for snuggling?" asked
Little Chick.

"No, she hasn't!"
said Tabby Kitten...

*"But when we curl up in our basket,
cosy and snug,
she washes my whiskers in a
warm tabby hug."*

Next Little Chick met
Furry Puppy digging in the
vegetable patch.

"Has your mum got feathery
wings for snuggling?" asked
Little Chick.

"No, she hasn't!"
said Furry Puppy...

*"But when we curl up in the kennel,
cosy and snug,
she licks my cold nose in a
warm, furry hug."*

Next Little Chick met
Woolly Lamb grazing among
the daisies.

"Has your mum got feathery
wings for snuggling?" asked
Little Chick.

"No she hasn't!"
said Woolly Lamb…

"But when we curl up under the oak tree,
cosy and snug,
she cuddles up close in a
warm, woolly hug."

Next Little Chick met
Hoppy Rabbit hopping by
the stream.

"Has your mum got feathery
wings for snuggling?" asked
Little Chick.

"No, she hasn't!"
said Hoppy Rabbit.

*"But when we curl up in the burrow,
cosy and snug,
she smooths my long ears in a
warm, hoppy hug."*

At last, Little Chick hurried
home to the henhouse.

"Welcome back, little one,"
said his mum. "Tell me what
you saw."

"I've seen lots of ways to snuggle,"
said Little Chick.
"But I still think feathery wings
are best – for chicken snuggles!"

And there in the henhouse,
cosy and snug,
they curled up together in a
warm, feathery hug!